Dear Parent:
Your child's love of reading starts here!

Every child learns to read in a different way and at his or her own speed. Some go back and forth between reading levels and read favorite books again and again. Others read through each level in order. You can help your young reader improve and become more confident by encouraging his or her own interests and abilities. From books your child reads with you to the first books he or she reads alone, there are I Can Read Books for every stage of reading:

SHARED READING
Basic language, word repetition, and whimsical illustrations, ideal for sharing with your emergent reader

BEGINNING READING
Short sentences, familiar words, and simple concepts for children eager to read on their own

READING WITH HELP
Engaging stories, longer sentences, and language play for developing readers

READING ALONE
Complex plots, challenging vocabulary, and high-interest topics for the independent reader

ADVANCED READING
Short paragraphs, chapters, and exciting themes for the perfect bridge to chapter books

I Can Read Books have introduced children to the joy of reading since 1957. Featuring award-winning authors and illustrators and a fabulous cast of beloved characters, I Can Read Books set the standard for beginning readers.

A lifetime of discovery begins with the magical words "I Can Read!"

Visit www.icanread.com for information
on enriching your child's reading experience.

For Sandra

Dirk Bones and the Mystery of the Missing Books Copyright © 2009 by Doug Cushman All rights reserved. No part of this book may be used or reproduced in any manner whatsoever without written permission except in the case of brief quotations embodied in critical articles and reviews. Printed in China. For information address HarperCollins Children's Books, a division of HarperCollins Publishers, 10 East 53rd Street, New York, NY 10022. www.harpercollinschildrens.com

Library of Congress Cataloging-in-Publication Data is available.
ISBN 978-0-06-073768-9 (trade bdg.)

10 11 12 13 SCP 10 9 8 7 6 5   ❖   First Edition

DIRK BONES

and the Mystery of the
Missing Books

story and pictures by
Doug Cushman

HarperCollins*Publishers*

KNOCK! KNOCK!

The door creaked open.

"Hello," I said.

"I am Dirk Bones,

a reporter for the newspaper

The Ghostly Tombs.

I am here to write a story

about Edgar Bleek,

the author of spooky books."

"That's me," said Edgar.

"Please come inside."

"My readers would like to know

where you get the ideas

for your stories," I said.

"The town of Ghostly

is very spooky," said Edgar.

"It gives me a lot to write about!"

"Do you have a new book?"

I asked.

"Yes," said Edgar.

"Let me show it to you.

I have the only copy

until it is in the bookstores."

We walked into his writing room.

Edgar looked on his desk.

"It's not here," he said.

"Maybe I misplaced it."

"I'll help you look for it,"

I said.

We looked in closets and cupboards,

in the bookcase and the bathtub.

But no book.

"Oh dear!" Edgar said.

"Do you think my book was stolen?"

"Maybe," I said.

I spied a wet leaf on the floor

next to the open window.

"This is a strange leaf," I said.

"It might be a clue

to the missing book.

Maybe I can find a picture of it

in a book at the library."

At the Ghostly Town Library
I looked through thirty-six books
of plants and leaves.
But I did not find one picture
of the strange leaf.

"What brings you here, Dirk?"
said Miss Elsa, the librarian.

"A mystery," I said.

"I have a mystery too," she said.

"Someone has been stealing books

from the library."

"What kind of books

have been stolen?" I asked.

"It's very odd," said Elsa.

"Only books by Edgar Bleek."

"Mr. Bleek has a book missing

from his house tonight," I said.

"Could someone have taken

all the books?"

"I also found this,"

Elsa said.

"It was next to the bookshelf."

She held up a leaf,

just like the one I found.

14

"These leaves are an important clue,"

I said.

"Maybe the bookstore

has books about plants.

I must solve this mystery!"

The bookstore was on

the other side of town.

I took a shortcut through

the Green Lagoon.

I walked through

the tall, wet grass.

Something moved in the water.

I turned.

A dark, dripping shape

climbed out of the lagoon.

It moved closer and closer. . . .

17

"ACHOO!"

"Bless you, Darlene," I said.

"My home is so wet,"

said Darlene.

"I always get the sniffles.

What are you doing here, Dirk?"

"Trying to solve a mystery," I said.

"Some books are missing."

"I have not seen any books,"

Darlene said,

"but lately I hear strange noises.

They sound like . . . voices!"

"Have you ever seen a leaf

like this?" I asked.

But Darlene did not answer.

"Yikes!" she cried.

She jumped back into the lagoon.

I turned to see a huge vine

rise out of the tall grass!

The vine was covered

with the strange leaves.

The vine slithered

like a big snake

into the town of Ghostly.

I ran after it.

It wriggled into the bookstore,

grabbed a book,

and slithered back to the lagoon.

It was *very* fast.

The vine disappeared.

I looked all around,

but the tall grass hid everything.

Just then I heard a sound.

It sounded like . . . a voice!

I followed the noise.

I pushed aside

a leafy bush and saw . . .

a plant holding a book!

It was *reading* the book!

The plant turned.

"Eek!" it said.

"You scared me!"

"You scared *me*!" I said.

"Who are you?"

"Lenore," said the plant.

"I'm a very rare

Creepus Crawler Talkus vine."

"Where do you come from?"

I asked.

"When I was a little seed
the wind blew me
from that faraway mountain,"
Lenore said.
"I planted myself here.
It's cool and wet,
perfect for my roots and leaves."

"Why are you stealing

books by Edgar Bleek?" I asked.

"I just borrowed them," said Lenore.

"I promise to give them back

after I read them to my children.

Mr. Bleek is their favorite author."

"Your *children*?" I asked.

I looked down.

Five little flowers popped up.

"We love spooky stories!" they said.

"This gives me an idea for a story

for my newspaper," I said.

The next day the front page read:

REPORTER GETS LIBRARY CARD FOR PLANT.

"Now my kids will always have

spooky stories," said Lenore.

"The library is the best place

for budding readers," said Edgar.

"Even budding flowers!" I said.